CW00516597

...rle was born in Cambridge in 1920 and was educated there at the Cambridge School of Art. On the outbreak of the Second World War he left his studies to serve in the Royal Engineers and in 1942 was captured by the Japanese at Singapore, then held by them for three and a half years. He is a hugely successful graphic artist and pictorial satirist. As well as his collaboration with Geoffrey Willans on the 'Molesworth' books and his invention of St Trinian's, his work has been the subject of numerous exhibitions across the world and appears in several major American and European collections. He moved to Paris in 1961 and then, in 1975, to a remote village in Haute-Provence, where he still lives.

Nicholas Lezard was born in London in 1963. He was Literary Editor of the *Modern Review*, and writes every week on books for the *Guardian* and on radio for the *Independent on Sunday*.

# RONALD SEARLE

## The Terror of St Trinian's

### and Other Drawings

*With an Introduction by Nicholas Lezard*

PENGUIN BOOKS

PENGUIN BOOKS

Published by the Penguin Group
Penguin Books Ltd, 27 Wrights Lane, London w8 5tz, England
Penguin Putnam Inc., 375 Hudson Street, New York, New York 10014, USA
Penguin Books Australia Ltd, Ringwood, Victoria, Australia
Penguin Books Canada Ltd, 10 Alcorn Avenue, Toronto, Ontario, Canada m4v 3b2
Penguin Books India (P) Ltd, 11, Community Centre, Panchsheel Park, New Delhi – 110 017, India
Penguin Books (NZ) Ltd, Private Bag 102902, NSMC, Auckland, New Zealand
Penguin Books (South Africa) (Pty) Ltd, 5 Watkins Street, Denver Ext 4, Johannesburg 2094, South Africa

Penguin Books Ltd, Registered Offices: Harmondsworth, Middlesex, England

This selection first published 2000
1

Copyright 1948, 1951, 1952, 1953, 1954, 1955, 1956 by Ronald Searle
Copyright © Ronald Searle, 1959
This selection copyright © Ronald Searle, 2000
All rights reserved

Printed in England by Clays Ltd, St Ives plc

# Contents

# *Acknowledgements*

The 'St Trinian's' drawings are taken from *Hurrah for St Trinian's* (1948), *Back to the Slaughterhouse* (1951), *The Terror of St Trinian's* (1952, with text by D. B. Wyndham Lewis) and *Souls in Torment* (1953). Other drawings (including the 'Hand of Authority' series) are taken from *Merry England, etc.* (1956). Use too has been made of the non-St Trinian's material in *Souls in Torment*. The 'Molesworth' drawings are taken from *Down With Skool!* (1953), *How to be Topp* (1954), *Whizz for Atomms* (1956) and *Back in the Jug Agane* (1959), all with text by Geoffrey Willans. *The Rake's Progress* (1955) is reproduced in its entirety.

# *Introduction*

Perhaps it is best to begin by admitting a minor, yet indulgent lapse in strict standards of editorial professionalism. There are a few of Ronald Searle's drawings that, strictly speaking, do not belong in this book. But we put them in anyway. Although Searle's 'Molesworth' drawings are reproduced fully (it should go without saying) in the Penguin Classics edition, we reproduce a few of them here, both at the series editor's insistence ('A Glurk Trolling') and mine ('grate latin lies'). We need hardly explain or apologize for their inclusion; but that we felt they *had* to go in, despite being duplicated elsewhere, says something about his appeal, the deep furrows he has made in the national consciousness.

Most people under forty came to Searle through the four 'Molesworth' books, his incredible collaboration with Geoffrey Willans, the novelist, teacher and wartime RNVS officer who found, in the depiction of the truculent, philosophical and rebellious schoolboy (a kind of Diogenes in shorts, with beetles doodled on his knees), his finest and most enduring creation. I first came to them as a schoolboy in the sixties and early seventies, in a prep school still faintly redolent of the cabbage-and-carbolic atmosphere of St Custard's. What struck me at the time was that the book was hardly an act of imagination; it was a documentary. We made allowances for the passage of history – the school was for day-bugs only, no one said '*cave*' at the approach of authority, and not all the masters were *quite* as demented – but the *mise-en-scène* was highly recognizable, authentic; we may even have willed our school to be a little more like St Custard's than it actually was, forcing life to live up to the world of art.

Much of Willans's linguistic exuberance passed us by – as far as we were concerned, he spelt 'strubres' more or less correctly – but it was Searle's illustrations that sealed the matter for us. For there, right on the page, was an example of how we felt we might be able to draw, had we the application or the energy. He was so expert and painstaking that we hardly recognized how expert and painstaking he was. He had managed to climb into a child's mind – strictly speaking, a boy's mind – and pull out our weirdest yet, at the same time, most standard imaginings. Most importantly, perhaps because we could see that he was not condescending, did not appear to be artistically slumming it, we knew at once that he was *on our side*, in that seemingly endless attritional war between adults and ourselves. If Willans exposed the grown-up world as a conspiracy against youth – and an inept and pointless conspiracy at that – then Searle's illustrations confirmed it, pitilessly, and in a visual language that we immediately understood.

It is also perhaps necessary to remind people now how rare it once was for schoolbooks to be illustrated, unless incompetently or emetically; and the molesworth books, which were, in a sense, schoolbooks, were more than just illustrated. Searle's contribution was not so much integral as essential for their success. The 'Molesworth' cycle burgeoned manically and generously with drawings, satisfying the schoolboy's craving for release from the tyranny of linear print. And the drawings were not dependent on the text; sometimes it seemed the other way round. There is no textual authority for many, if not most, of the illustrations; the word 'illustration' is, in this context, misleading. The molesworth-headed spider ('closer and closer, crept the ghastly THING') just leaps into the book, as a boy's vicious daydream interrupts a period of great tedium, most typically, as I recall, Latin lessons. The 'grate latin lies', also an autonomous series of cartoons, said not only all that needed to be said about the supposed classical ideal, they also said everything that needed to be said about the timelessly disappointing nature of the human condition. Take 'All the romans loved home', with the browbeaten centurion still in his armour, the mocking image of an authority he can never command in his own home, the wife yelling at some prior incompetence or dereliction, the child crying at some prior and presumably imaginary or trifling injustice, even the dog pinching his dinner; the man's resigned, exhausted slump not only that of someone trapped in history, but a horribly proleptic vision of the destiny that awaited those foolish enough to grow up. It told us all, in the blink of time it took the eye to register the details, what was wrong with the nuclear family, the thankless tedium of duty, at the same time as the conventional culture all around sang the praises of the homestead. It was a highly concentrated and dyspeptic sitcom, but – and this is the mystery and spirit of cartoon art – it was still funny. It made me laugh then, and, now that I am however strangely happily in that centurion's caligulae, more or less, it makes me laugh even more.

But when young, in those days, one felt that merely to hold a book with such a number of illustrations was a signal of rebellion in itself; we felt obscurely that Searle's drawings begged authoritarian disapproval simply by existing in such profusion. That they also flayed their subjects with a merciless and unforgiving line – both grotesque and precise, one never looked at the world the same way after his illustrations as one did before – made it all the better. That it was done with such sympathetic relish made it even better than that. Parents were embarrassing, hypocritical cretins, either callous in the victory of worldly success, or living pitiable lives of continual defeat; schoolmasters incompetent frauds, either grasping, sottish, brutal, ignorant or half-dead. Searle got them *just right*. We learned, through this astonishing partnership between text and pictures, the incontrovertible urgency of satire.

And in that we see the circular, autophagic compulsion of the satirist. The world is horrible; but without the horror the satirist would be out of a job. It is necessary that the satirist does not make it a better place. This can drive them mad; Swift predicted as much of himself, and he was right. Searle, however, has not been driven mad, precisely because of the medium he works in, which is low enough in the conventionally accepted artistic hierarchy to escape either serious and damaging scrutiny or pontification; and, crucially, it makes us laugh. This is a matter of almost tiresome obviousness but it is important. The cadaverous bookseller who asks the invisible purchaser – us? – whether he or she wants *The Anatomy of Melancholy* wrapped up 'or will you read it now?' is in itself (as Burton intended his own work to be) a cure for melancholy, yet acknowledging the fundamental justness of the bookseller's position. It also bespeaks a strange satisfaction with one's own gloomy view of the world – that one just *can't wait* to read *The Anatomy of Melancholy*. (I would not be surprised to learn that Searle was handed the cartoon on a plate, as it were, by an event in real life.)

Searle's laughter has something heroic in it: he may expose his subjects as figures of fun, but there is in this an implicit gratitude that such
people have persisted,[1] despite the artist's knowing, eternal gaze, and
against their better judgement (that is, had they any such to speak of), in
their dreams of success. Hence his sequence of drawings for his own
Rakes' Progresses, where instead of a Hogarthian denunciation of indol-
ence and vice, he mocks instead the aspirations of those deemed worthy
by society: the politician, the doctor, the poet; the most tenderly observed
is, paradoxically, the incompetent Master of Foxhounds, continually
breaking his collarbone (that most ludic and trifling of injuries) and in the
end mourned by a pack, if that is the word, of baying foxes.

We know this is satire, and not pasquinade, because so much of it still
works. We might not get all the references, but their surroundings still jolt
us with their timeless perspicacity. (The politician's downfall: 'Encouraged by success expresses an opinion. Cast out by whips. Expelled from
Party.') Some have been waiting to be fulfilled: the St Trinian's girl being
exhorted, while injecting a competitor with a tranquillizer, to fair play:
'always use a clean needle.'

Searle was born, in 1920, in Cambridge, into a socially anonymous background, where male children were expected to be clerks or minor civil
servants. Placed almost squarely in the middle of society, he had the ideal
vantage point from which to observe his country, without having to
suffer the distortion of an undue affection for his origins. It is an easy
background to shrug off if you know what you want to do with yourself,
and Searle did know, from an early age. In his introduction to *Ronald
Searle in Perspective* (1984), he wrote:

Quite suddenly I began to draw. I had been scribbling for ever. Now it took shape
and I became, first fascinated, then obsessed, with what it was possible to do with
pen and pencil. No one paid much attention to this, nor to the fact that the drawings were immediately grotesque. This was assumed to be one of the penalties for
being 'cackhanded', local dialect for mocking a left-hander, which is what I am.

[1] In Paris, Searle met, and drew, another poet of persistence in the face of absurdity, Samuel
Beckett; Searle was highly impressed, it would seem, and, using a Beckettian turn of phrase
himself, described the writer as the most 'unwarpable' of his subjects.

It was my good fortune that I got off to such a suitable geographical start. I had the inborn advantage of the eccentric, the abnormal seeming to me, as well as to most of those around me, perfectly normal and not at all a caricature of 'proper' behaviour as demanded by 'them' from outside. In addition, nobody suggested that there was anything ludicrous in the fact that, for the first time since the Searles had plodded their way through the bogs to escape the Vikings, a left-handed Searle was proclaiming that he had to be An Artist, instead of a gravedigger, or whatever.

(Like a surprising number of artists, he is a good writer.)

He started, like most cartoonists, as an artist, that is, trained (in his case by the Cambridge School of Art) to draw things as they were.[2] His early cartoons are not yet Searlesque, if that is the word. At some point the artist gives way to the caricaturist, who draws things as they are superficially not. His development as an artist has to take into account his wartime record, from his volunteering for the army in April 1939 until his liberation from the squalor of Changi Gaol in 1945. He had been a prisoner of war since 1942, in among the most wretched and soul-destroying of situations a soldier could experience. More often than not it was the body that was destroyed, rather than just the soul. It is probably tasteless to speculate that it was during his imprisonment by the Japanese that his vision was served by watching the bodies of his fellow soldiers become emaciated caricatures of their former selves; at great personal risk to himself, he created a visual record, hundreds of sketches drawn in secrecy and concealed beneath the bodies of cholera victims, which his Japanese captors were disinclined to handle. Of himself, in October 1943, after the completion of the Siam–Burma railway, he wrote:

I weighed about seven of my former eleven stone, my leaf-bound legs were puffed up with beri-beri, large areas of my body were decorated with a suppurating crust from some exotic skin disease and one of my ankles was eaten to the bone by a large tropical ulcer. Apart from this, my three-weekly bouts of malaria had left what was still visible of my skin between scabies and ringworm, a pleasing bright

[2] 'At the Cambridge Art School it was drummed into us that we should not move, eat, drink or sleep without a sketchbook in the hand.' R.S., 1977.

yellow. However medically picturesque I may have been, behind the mess I was still alive and just about kicking.

Changi Gaol, where he was finally to be imprisoned, had been, he noted sardonically, built by the British.

It epitomized – and probably still does – all that is administratively desirable for degrading and psychologically diminishing the guilty, in the firm belief that confinement for a number of years in small locked boxes can be spiritually re-habilitating and physically cleansing both for them and for society.

It had been designed for six hundred criminals; by the time Searle arrived, it contained ten thousand. Not only hungry but desperate for something to smoke, he would use spare corners of his drawings, 'half of *Pickwick Papers* after a fifth reading, and the whole of Rose Macaulay's *Minor Pleasures of Life*'. He met Macaulay many years later by chance.

I told her I had been able to add a further minor pleasure to her anthology. Sad to say she was not amused, looked me up and down with distaste and turned her back to talk to someone more respectful. Dickens, I feel, would have been more understanding.

Once the war was over, he drew on his experience of captivity only tangentially. In his 1990 biography of Searle, Russell Davies points out the obvious similarity between the 'bloody sportsdays' illustration for *Lilliput* of 1952 (St Trinian's girls chained to a heavy roller, being whipped by a sadistic schoolmistress) and '"Light Duties" for sick men', a drawing made in 1944 of prisoners pulling a heavy roller while being overseen by a Japanese guard. 'This is one of the few instances in which the Changi experience can be seen to have a directly circumstantial bearing on Searle's black humour,' says Davies, who also points out that the whip-wielding mistress is an aberration in the logic of St Trinian's, where staff and pupils are on the same side, as in Beachcomber's Narkover.[3]

---

[3] Searle put the situation at St Trinian's like this, in 1972, to a would-be adapter of the Trinian's cycle to the musical stage: 'The Staff, behind an extremely old-fashioned façade, conceal equivalent excesses and plenty of lesbianism. They insist on good manners at all times, and in all circumstances, but are extremely tolerant. Even to the point of employing an abortionist-nurse to look after the school crèche, and care for the girls' babies while their mothers are busy in the school lab, refining heroin base.'

I don't think much need be made of this: he suffered horrors, and may be felt to have dwelt on them enough at the time. Besides, he was to pay due homage to his comrades in his 1984 exhibition and book, *To the Kwai and Back*, which contains a good selection of his wartime drawings. (But not the relatively lighthearted cartoons he drew at the time, suitable enough for *Punch*; these figure in the biography, along with one drawing, in which various dishes, labelled from A to Z, are yearningly pictured; an idea, or an echo, of this is given in the improbably lavish banquet shown being eaten by a mother and father on page 92 of the Penguin *Molesworth*. Caption: 'I think sometimes parents may wonder whether we are worth the sacrifices they make for us.')

What his war did to his politics we can only guess at. He has kept fairly silent on the subject, allowing us to hopefully infer rather than straightforwardly deduce. He joined the army in April 1939, in a way that even left-leaning intellectuals and artists of the time did not. He gives no reasons in *To the Kwai and Back*. He was not a member of the privileged classes by any means, but not *lumpenproletariat* either; it is probable that he was an early volunteer against fascism rather than for the army, and while for all I know there have been many interviews with him in which he has said as much, as far as I have seen he has been reticent on the subject. He was, over all, an artist. But artists, as we understand the term, do not often sign up for active service. Can we glimpse his attitude in the section of *The Rake's Progress* devoted to The Poet, where the hero both signs up for the International Brigades yet finds himself strangely captivated by the prominent buttocks of the young men in the Hitler Youth? It's certainly just a dig at Spender, not at all earthed by Spender's caricature further into the sequence. He has said that one work that changed his artistic direction was Marcel Ray's monograph on George Grosz, and, *mutatis mutandis*, there are occasions when he draws very much like an English Grosz, that is, a Grosz living in a society whose hypocrisy is more genteel than murderous.

Post-war, his career flourished. (I refer readers who want chapter and verse to Russell Davies's excellent biography.) Someone with a good graphic hand is never in as dire danger of starvation as a writer. He looks, in photographs, like the kind of semi-bohemian artist he occasionally ribs gently in his work, goateed, wearing turtle-necks and a lot of black; he had, for the times, an unconventional love life. But you cannot deduce from this an attitude of relentless and all-embracing anti-conformity. He subscribes neither to the class struggle nor to the vested interests of the gentry, and from time to time has taken pot-shots at each, happy to ridicule upwardly mobile Trades Unionists as well as Tories. The Trade Union Leader's downfall in the *Rake's Progress* series has the rubric 'Knighted. Weeps at Party Conference. Cries "these hands are worker's hands."' A cartoon in *Tribune* of 1949 shows a tiny, goateed Searle sketching at the Conservative Party conference while a pop-eyed, sclerotic Tory glares at him; the caption: 'By God – if I had a horsewhip I'd horsewhip 'im.' Another *Tribune* cartoon of 1951 shows a fur-coated *grande dame* carrying a nasty-looking peke, asking a fed-up-looking butcher: 'You stand there, talking about fair shares, without under- standing the basic rules of humanity. How do you expect my little dog to live?' (At the same time, he was contributing to the *Sunday Express*; but then so did the notionally much more left-wing Carl Giles.) He was contributing to *Punch*, *Tribune*, the *SE*, *Lilliput*, *Circus*, *Seven* and *Our Time* ('ephemeral magazines of the left', in Davies's phrase). He was capable of producing, around Suez, some quite shameful anti-Nasser propaganda leaflets, at the request of an old friend, Brigadier Bernard Fergusson, who recruited him for the Psychological Warfare Department.

The St Trinian's drawings, with a text by D. B. Wyndham Lewis, became a huge success; and an imprisoning one; interviewed by a young Quentin Blake for the BBC in 1951 he was already intimating that he had had enough. Perhaps St Trinian's was too much of a one-joke routine; but they encouraged his publisher, Max Parrish, to insist that whatever was done as a follow-up should have 'profuse' illustrations. As indeed it – *Down With Skool!* – did.

This selection stops at the time he left this country for France, where he has lived ever since, and it is not the business of this introduction to speculate or air his reasons for leaving. The cartoons here, although sketches of a vanished age, deal with subjects archetypal enough not to demand a thorough glossary. This volume marks an acknowledgement of Searle's place in the national culture, the doodles he has scrawled in the collective mind. Which is not to suggest that his art is itself somehow less than art. He knew exactly what he was dealing with when he dealt with the subject itself. 'The Painter' from *The Rake's Progress* inspired a letter from Sir Alfred Munnings, Past President of the RA, which was headed 'Dear *Artist*', the word 'artist' underlined three times. That should settle that.

Cartoonists are not nearly given their due in this country. They encourage condescension or scorn not only by the deliberate pitch of their art – calculatedly low, demotic – but also by the very fact of their often prodigious fertility, the way it looks as though they can knock things out, day after day (everyone, throughout their lives, has had a few ideas for cartoons, and so knows how difficult it must be to do it full-time). Searle's line tickles the boundary between cartooning and art. The line, particularly when describing the human body, wavers between plausible, expressionistic distortion and outright freakishness. They are somehow both rudimentary and detailed, both busy and sparse at once; you can't even be sure whether he drew them freehand or with guide-lines. It is a style that's both completely original and completely familiar, in a way that is entirely self-sufficient, and a continuing inspiration and influence to this day, and beyond.

Nicholas Lezard

*St Trinian's*

'Owing to the international situation the match with St Helen's
has been postponed.'

'Girls, girls! – A little less noise, please.'

'Well that's OK – now for old "Stinks".'

'And you, Sylvia ffinch-ffrench-ffinch ...'

Angela Menace, with the battle-light in her eyes

'You fascinating swine'

'Playing with lethal weapons – a boy of your age!'

'Bash her again. I think she moved.'

'Caught the little beast trying to warn Herbert Morrison.'

'Well done, Cynthia – it *was* Deadly Nightshade.'

'Chuck those out – they're harmless.'

'But, Miss Merryweather, you *said* we could bring our pets back with us.'

'Fair play, St Trinian's – use a clean needle.'

'And this is Rachel – our head girl.'

'Smashing! – now pass the bat's blood.'

'Go on, make him abolish prep.'

'Come along, prefects. Playtime over.'

'Don't be greedy, Cynthia, give your sister some.'

'Little Maisy's our problem child.'

'Could you tell me the time, please?'

'Eunice, dear – aren't we rather muddling our patron saints?'

The Tenth Birthday party: 'Honestly, darling, you don't look a
day over nine.'

'Elspeth! – Put that back *AT ONCE.*'

'Ruddy sportsdays …'

'Some little girl didn't hear me say "unarmed combat".'

'Cleaners getting slack, Horsefall'

R. Searle reviews his troops

The End

*from* Merry England, etc.

"Flippin' Mithras heads."

beware

Come fill the Cup, and in the Fire of Spring
The Winter Garment of Repentance fling:
  The Bird of Time has but a little way
To fly – and Lo! the Bird is on the Wing.

                              Omar khayyám

Ronald Searle 1955.

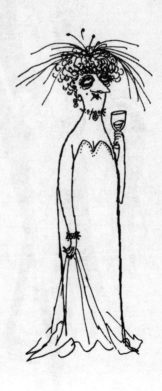

'Unaccountable thing, heredity ...'

The Child-hater

'I say, I think its going to clear.'

'Looks like mutiny …'

*The Hand of Authority*

*from* Souls in Torment

SMITHS
for Crisps
TAKE SOME
HOME WITH YOU

The book of
the film of
the book

WHS

A Book
worth for
LAUGHS

Ronald Searle

"One *Vogue*, one *Art and Industry*, one *Pond Keeper and Aquarist*, one *Health and Strength* ..."

"Shall I wrap it up or will you read it now?"

"Read any good books lately?"

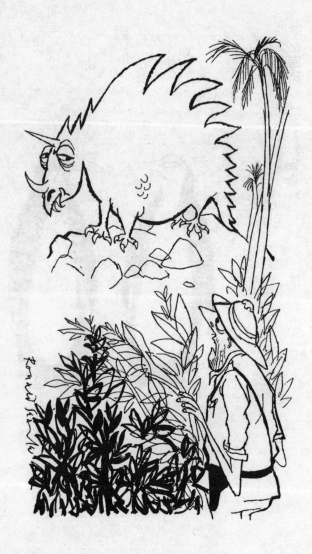

"My God – Roget's Thesaurus!"

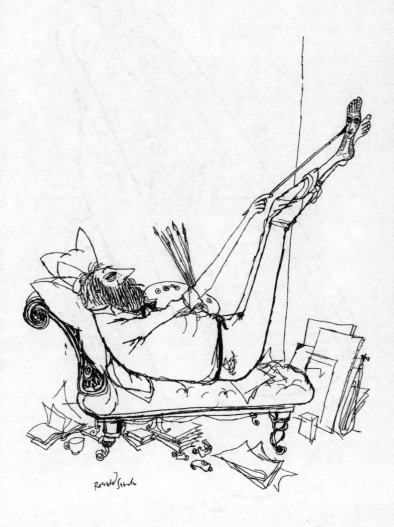

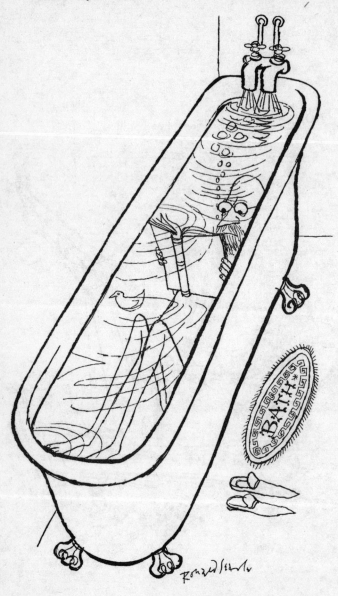

Molesworth

## KANES I HAVE KNOWN BY N. MOLESWORTH

1 'Old Faithful'. Whippy, no ferrule, 'palm-tree' ends. Can be thrown for dogs to fetch in the holidays.

2 The 'Nonpliant' or 'Rigid' with silencer attachment to drown victims cries.

3 'Creaker' or split-seam. For use by 'hurt-me-more-than-it-hurts-you' kaners.

4 The first weapon he can lay hands on.

5 The 'Caber', Scotch-type for senior boys.

6 The hair-fine specialists kane for marksmen. Fitted with telescopic sights and range finder.

## KNOW THE ENEMY OR MASTERS AT A GLANCE

I cannot keep order.

The boys all look on me as a friend

I am hoping to get a job in the colonial service somewhere.

I am keen on the latest developments in education.

I advise you strongly not to start ragging *me*.

You may think I'm soft but I'm hard, damned hard.

Mr Chips? No such character ever existed.

And when I asked him the supine stem of confiteor the fool didn't know.

I may not know much but I am jolly good at football.

No. The spirit of tolerance, you fool.

The crested grebes are mating!

I am still hoping for a job in the colonial service somewhere

I was sent by the agency at the last minute before term began

A joke's a joke chaps but don't go too far

## TABLE OF GRIPS AND TORTURES
## FOR MASTERS

The plain blip for numskulls

Side hair tweak exquisitely painful

Single-hair extraction for non-attenders

The cork in the storm for violent temperaments

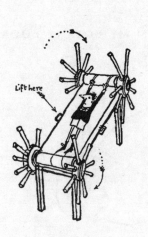

Portable rack for maths masters
(with thumbscrew attachment)

The headshave with ruler

The Cumberland creep from
behind with silver pencil

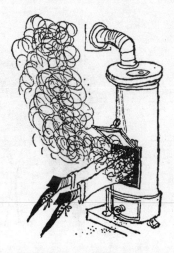

The simple open furnace

## FRAGRANT LEAVES FROM MY BOTANY BOOK

A Glurk Trolling.

A Blue-nosed Chuck Brooding.

A Lesser Titwort Avoiding a Worm.

A Mongolian Thick Surprised (Rear View.)

## PARENTS AT A GLANCE

I always think character is more important than brains.

But we *always* give him gin!

I've brought him some chocs, a comic, an air gun, a pound of Turkish Delight and can he come home next Wednesday?

When I was a boy we got six of the best every day. Made me what I am.

And what's behind this wee
door?

No darling Schopenhauer did not
*quite* mean that.

I don't care if Mrs Bradbury did
run for Britain I'm still going to
have a cocktail.

I am sorry about his vest and pants
but when he was a little boy he
always wore combinations.

I think sometimes parents may wonder whether we are worth the sacrifices they make for us.

# THE PRIVATE LIFE OF THE GERUND

The Gerund attacks some peaceful pronouns

Kennedy discovers the gerund and leads it back into captivity

A greund shut out. No place for it in one of my sentences

Social snobbery. A gerund 'cuts' a gerundive

## GRATE LATIN LIES

The customs of the Gauls were honourable

Great crimes were rare in ancient times

The girls were beautiful

All the Romans love home

Gabbitas creeps round the wood one way

Thring creeps round the other way

Gabbitas and Thring trap a young man and lead him off to be a master

Trap for dere Santa

'Nearer and nearer crept the ghastly THING'

Come on grab him by the neck scrag him give a chinese burn beat him

g Fifth dynasty? You surprise me

The molesworth/pearson portable roving eye have one serious defeckt

*The Rake's Progress*

*The Rake's Progress*

THE ATHLETE

1. Promise

Wins egg and spoon race at Central School sports. Takes job in cement factory. Romps home in works paper chase. Mentioned in House Magazine

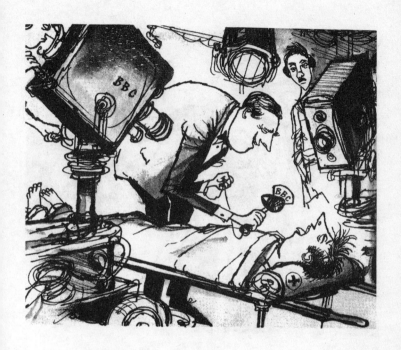

## 2. Success

Joins Fulham Athletic Club. Paces crack miler in attempt on world record. Praised for selflessness. Appears in *In Town Tonight*

3. Triumph

Wins Mile of Century in Olympic Games. Laps ageing Zatapek in Bucharest. Edits *Boys' Book of Athletics*. Marries Australian hurdler

4. Temptation

Paid £50 to sponsor underwear advertisement. Suspended by AAA. Visits States. Accepts athletic scholarship at Yale

## 5. Downfall

Tries Baseball. Tries Rounders. Too old at 30. Sells Olympic
Medal. Returns to England as a stoker on a Guano boat

## 6. Ruin

Plight revealed by article in the *News of the World*. Offered
night-watchman's job in Durham. Runs for train. Expires

*The Rake's Progress*

THE GIRLFRIEND

1. Emergence

Famous at Cambridge for her affectionate nature. Rusticated.
Interests herself in Social Welfare

2. Success

Outstanding success at Fabian Summer School

3. Temptation

Befriends politicians. Subscribes to *Hansard*. Persuaded to stand for Parliament

### 4. Triumph

Elected with large majority. Cancels subscription to *Mother and Home*

5. Downfall

Stamina at all-night sittings attracts ministerial attention. Under-Secretary to Ministry of Defence

6. Ruin

Guest of the Week on *Woman's Hour*. Minister of Health. Profile in *The Lady*. DBE

*The Rake's Progress*

THE SOLDIER

1914

Sword of Honour and Carruthers Prize for Scripture and Old
Testament Map-reading

1916

Kills five Huns with a broken sabre. DSO, Croix de Guerre (avec Palme). Kissed by Foch

1922

Inspired by Capt. Liddell Hart leaves army to write on airborne tactics. Photograph in *Army Quarterly*

1938

Military adviser to Secretary of State for War. Secures adoption
of a new greatcoat. Starts memoirs

1940

War Office. Appointed Director General of ABCA. Wounded. Retires with Rank of Lieut.-General

1948

Chairman of Committee to advise on colour schemes for railway
waiting-rooms. Knocked down by a taxi at St Pancras. Expires

*The Rake's Progress*

THE POET

1. Genesis

Discovers *The Waste Land*. First verse play published in *The Cherwell*. Drafts autobiography

2. Emergence

Captivated by German Youth Movement. Settles in Berlin.
Shakes hands with W. H. Auden and Christopher Isherwood.
Deported

## 3. Success

Joins International Brigade. Barcelona. Sunstroke. Converted to Yoga. Reads own poems at Kingsway Hall

4. Temptation

Dines with Cyril Connolly. Special issue of *Horizon* devoted to tone poems. Shakes hands with Stephen Spender

5. Downfall

Dirge, accompanied by Tongan nose flutes, broadcast on Third
Programme. British Council lecture tour of Friendly Islands.
Nods to C. Day Lewis

6. Ruin

Accepts Chair of Poetry at a Los Angeles girls' college. Visits
Aldous Huxley. Succumbs to Mescalin

*The Rake's Progress*

THE TRADE UNION LEADER

1. Promise

Joins Union as apprentice. Blacks eye of non-Union lad. Praised by Father of the Chapel

2. Fulfilment

Leads famous 'Bob-a-Nob' march. Accused of wrecking Empire
by the *Daily Mail*

3. Success

National Organiser. Joins 'Popular Front' agitation. Has a drink with Mr Pollitt. Weds

4. Temptation

Elected General Secretary of the Union. Buys first dress suit

5. Downfall

Knighted. Weeps at Party Conference. Cries 'these are worker's hands'. Has autobiography 'ghosted'

6. Ruin

Refused American visa. Blacks eye of embassy clerk.
International indignation. Takes slow boat to China

*The Rake's Progress*

THE ACTOR

1. Overture

A bonny lad, but witless. Shines in fit-up tour of *Private Lives*. Sends press cuttings to Old Vic. Gets them back. Complains to Equity

2. Success

Finds old *Stage* in the Salisbury – lands job with Donald Wolfit. Spotted by talent scout. Praised by Harold Hobson. Flown to Hollywood

3. Triumph

Doctor Johnson in musical version of Boswell. Oscar. Life Story in *Collier's*. Man of distinction. Sends donation to Old Vic

4. Temptation

On location in Capri with prominent Continental starlet. Weds. Immediate offers from Jack Hylton and Old Vic. Chooses Old Vic

## 5. Downfall

Insists on Lear. Underplays in American accent. Ivor Brown
carried out screaming. Divorced for mental cruelty

6. Ruin

Sells ex-wife's life-story to *Reveille*. Starts own repertory
company. Reserve Hoop-la attendant at Theatrical Garden
Party

*The Rake's Progress*

THE PAINTER

## 1. Genesis

Scholarship to the Royal College of Art. First efforts praised by Mr Darwin

2. Recognition

Designs tableau for the Chelsea Arts Ball. First painting
exhibited at the Tea Centre

3. Success

Discovers Banana Motif. One-man exhibition (on a banana motif) sells out. Praised by Sir John Rothenstein

4. Triumph

Commissioned to paint Lady Docker in gold leaf.
Praised by Sir Alfred Munnings

## 5. Downfall

Expelled from the London Group. Paints Lady Munnings' dog.
ARA

6. Ruin

Televised sitting next to Sir Winston at RA banquet.
RA. Knighted

*The Rake's Progress*

THE DON

1. Advent

Born in an almshouse in Middlesbrough of poor but
honest parents

## 2. Triumph

Major scholarship to Oxford

3. Temptation

Fellow of All Souls. Invited to write a column for the
*Daily Mirror*

4. Glory

Outspoken views lead to national reputation on TV. Quiz programmes

5. Downfall

Insulting Gilbert Harding leads to expulsion from Lime Grove.
Spurned by his friends

6. Ruin

Fails to make a comeback in *Reynolds News*. Dies in penury on the doorstep of *Everybody's Weekly*

*The Rake's Progress*

THE DRAMATIC CRITIC

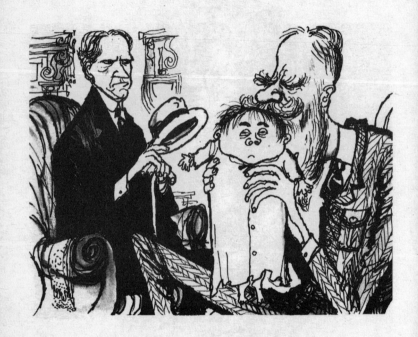

1. Prologue

Kissed by Bernard Shaw when young in the presence of
Granville Barker. Inspired

2. Emergence

Produces Othello in bathing costumes for the OUDS.
Praised by *Isis*. Bad notice in *The Times*

3. Recognition

Suggests that *The Times* critic retires in favour of a more contemporary approach. Offer declined. Piqued

## 4. Success

Joins *Reveille*. Writes slashing attack on the state of Dramatic Criticism today. Immediately signed up by Popular Daily. Thrilled

## 5. Triumph

Meteoric success. Banned by West End theatres for kindness
to Hannen Swaffer. Expelled from The Caprice. Nervous
breakdown

## 6. Downfall

Brilliantly restrained comeback with BBC Critics. Drama
Adjustor Arts Council. Treasurer Critics' Circle. Respected

*The Rake's Progress*

THE DOCTOR

## 1. Advent

Deeply moved by incidence of Dropped Arches among
the working classes. Becomes dedicated student

## 2. Success

Brilliant graduate. MRCP, FRCS, MCOGS. First paper
in *The Lancet* quoted by *Time and Tide*

3. Triumph

Enormous practice in the Rhondda Valley. Combats foot and mouth disease. Beloved by all

4. Reward

Undermined by constant night calls. Develops Night Starvation

## 5. Temptation

In sanatorium writes blackleg magazine series on slipped discs. Sensational success. Receives autographed photo from A. J. Cronin

6. Downfall

Resigns from BMA. Joins *Tribune* as medical correspondent.
Stoned in Harley Street. Leaves body to science

*The Rake's Progress*

THE MP

1. Advent

Born of rich but honest parents. Fired with political
enthusiasm by radical Norland Nurse

## 2. Emergence

Secretary Cambridge Union Society. Contests hopeless seat with
great verve. Bloody – but unbowed

### 3. Success

Wins bye-election. Moderation of views brings frequent
bookings on BBC Political Forum

4. Triumph

Smiled at by Prime Minister. PPS

5. Temptation

Encouraged by success expresses an opinion. Cast out by Whips.
Expelled from Party

6. Ruin

Praised by *News Chronicle.* Joins Liberal Shadow Cabinet.
Divorced

*The Rake's Progress*

THE CLERGYMAN

1. Advent

Inspired (and muscular) East End vicar. Dedicates himself
to reform Church of England

2. Success

Organises mass meeting to demand Disestablishment
and Expulsion of bishops from the House of Lords

3. Triumph

Hits headlines. Televised. Nationwide interest. 'Health'
at complimentary dinner organised by Crockfords

4. Temptation

Nominated Bishop of Woolchester. Elected to Athenaeum.
Introduced to convivial and sporting pleasures

## 5. Downfall

Goes incognito to Kempton Park during sessions of
Convocation. Spotted by Archbishop on TV newsreel

6. Ruin

Rocket from Lambeth. Resigns bishopric. Takes soapbox
to Orators' Corner. Bursts blood vessel. Passes over

*The Rake's Progress*

THE NOVELIST

1. Advent

Son of a North Country toiler. Writes authentic novel in dialect
on the backs of old envelopes between teabreaks. Sacked

2. Triumph

Book published. Immediate success. Acclaimed Foyles
Literary Luncheon. Mobbed in W. H. Smith's, Clapham

3. Glory

Second novel chosen as Book at Bedtime. Bats for Authors at National Book League cricket match. Stage rights of first book bought for Wilfred Pickles

4. Temptation

Name unfamiliar to John Lehmann at PEN Club party.
Thenceforth tormented by desire to get into *New Writing*.
Moves to Paris

5. Downfall

Critical analysis of J. P. Sartre rejected by *London Magazine* and *Encounter*. Sales of third novel sink to 750 copies*

* including British Commonwealth

6. Ruin

Psychopathic treatment for schizophrenia. Emigrates to Australia.
Revered

*The Rake's Progress*

THE HUMOURIST

1. Germination

Readily responds to tickling. Fond of practical jokes.
Loses two fingers

## 2. Recognition

Lampoons masters in margins of school books. Beaten.
Satirizes Dons in *Cambridge Review*. Sent down

3. Success

Contributes three monologues to a Watergate Review.
Four writs for libel

## 4. Triumph

Ridicules the Law in the *Sunday Dispatch*. Jailed. Becomes National Figure. Invited to write for *Punch*. Becomes National Institution

## 5. Downfall

First Resident Comedian BBC Third Programme.
Hon. D. Litt (Cambridge). Buys country house

6. Ruin

Attempts to be Life and Soul of the Athenaeum. Knighted.
Succumbs to melancholia

*The Rake's Progress*

THE MASTER OF FOXHOUNDS

1. Promise

Serious fall off rocking-horse. Breaks collar-bone

## 2. Success

Photographed by *Tatler* riding in Grind at Oxford. Elated.
Takes the Heythrop. Breaks collar-bone

## 3. Triumph

Parades hounds at Lord Mayor's Show. Judges hunters at White City. Trips over Duke of Beaufort. Breaks collar bone

4. Temptation

Runs fox to ground in neighbouring county. Starts digging.
Spotted by rival MFH. Reported

5. Downfall

Expelled from Masters of Foxhounds Association. Takes to drink.
Thrown out of Hunt Ball. Breaks collar-bone

## 6. Ruin

Fails to renew subscription to *Horse and Hound*. Gets job
as Pest Officer, East Anglia. Falls off bicycle. Breaks neck

*The Rake's Progress*

THE GREAT LOVER

'Why don't you let down your hair or something?'

The End

# READ MORE IN PENGUIN

In every corner of the world, on every subject under the sun, Penguin represents quality and variety – the very best in publishing today.

For complete information about books available from Penguin – including Puffins, Penguin Classics and Arkana – and how to order them, write to us at the appropriate address below. Please note that for copyright reasons the selection of books varies from country to country.

**In the United Kingdom**: Please write to *Dept. EP, Penguin Books Ltd, Bath Road, Harmondsworth, West Drayton, Middlesex UB7 0DA*

**In the United States**: Please write to *Consumer Sales, Penguin Putnam Inc., P.O. Box 12289 Dept. B, Newark, New Jersey 07101-5289.* VISA and MasterCard holders call 1-800-788-6262 to order Penguin titles

**In Canada**: Please write to *Penguin Books Canada Ltd, 10 Alcorn Avenue, Suite 300, Toronto, Ontario M4V 3B2*

**In Australia**: Please write to *Penguin Books Australia Ltd, P.O. Box 257, Ringwood, Victoria 3134*

**In New Zealand**: Please write to *Penguin Books (NZ) Ltd, Private Bag 102902, North Shore Mail Centre, Auckland 10*

**In India**: Please write to *Penguin Books India Pvt Ltd, 11 Community Centre, Panchsheel Park, New Delhi 110017*

**In the Netherlands**: Please write to *Penguin Books Netherlands bv, Postbus 3507, NL-1001 AH Amsterdam*

**In Germany**: Please write to *Penguin Books Deutschland GmbH, Metzlerstrasse 26, 60594 Frankfurt am Main*

**In Spain**: Please write to *Penguin Books S. A., Bravo Murillo 19, 1° B, 28015 Madrid*

**In Italy**: Please write to *Penguin Italia s.r.l., Via Benedetto Croce 2, 20094 Corsico, Milano*

**In France**: Please write to *Penguin France, Le Carré Wilson, 62 rue Benjamin Baillaud, 31500 Toulouse*

**In Japan**: Please write to *Penguin Books Japan Ltd, Kaneko Building, 2-3-25 Koraku, Bunkyo-Ku, Tokyo 112*

**In South Africa**: Please write to *Penguin Books South Africa (Pty) Ltd, Private Bag X14, Parkview, 2122 Johannesburg*

# READ MORE IN PENGUIN

**Money**  Martin Amis

John Self, consumer extraordinaire, makes deals, spends wildly and does reckless movie-world business, all the while grabbing everything he can to sate his massive appetites: alcohol, tobacco, pills, junk food and more. This is a tale of life lived without restraint; of money, the terrible things it can do and the disasters it can precipitate. 'Terribly, terminally funny: laughter in the dark, if ever I heard it' *Guardian*

**The Big Sleep and Other Novels**  Raymond Chandler

Raymond Chandler created the fast-talking, trouble-seeking Californian private eye Philip Marlowe for his first great novel, *The Big Sleep*. Marlowe's entanglement with the Sternwood family is the background to a story reflecting all the tarnished glitter of the great American Dream. 'One of the greatest crime writers, who set standards that others still try to attain' *Sunday Times*

**In Cold Blood**  Truman Capote

Controversial and compelling, *In Cold Blood* reconstructs the murder in 1959 of a Kansas farmer, his wife and both their children. The book that made Capote's name is a seminal work of modern prose, a synthesis of journalistic skill and powerfully evocative narrative. 'The American dream turning into the American nightmare ... a remarkable book' *Spectator*

**The Town and the City**  Jack Kerouac

The town is Galloway in New England, birthplace of the five sons and three daughters of the Martin family in the early 1900s. The city is New York, the vast and heaving melting pot which lures them all in search of a future and an identity. Inspired by grief over his father's death, and his own determination to write the Great American Novel, *The Town and the City* is an essential prelude to Jack Kerouac's later classics.

# READ MORE IN PENGUIN

*Published or forthcoming:*

**Love in a Cold Climate and Other Novels**   Nancy Mitford

Nancy Mitford's brilliantly witty, irreverent stories of the upper classes in pre-war London and Paris conjure up a world of glamour and decadence, in which her heroines deal with hilariously eccentric relatives, the excitement of love and passion, and the thrills of the Season. But beneath their glittering surfaces, Nancy Mitford's novels are also hymns to a lost era and to the brevity of life and love.

**The Prime of Miss Jean Brodie**   Muriel Spark

Romantic, heroic, comic and tragic, schoolmistress Jean Brodie has become an iconic figure in post-war fiction. Her glamour, freethinking ideas and manipulative charm hold dangerous sway over her girls at the Marcia Blaine Academy, who are introduced to a privileged world of adult games that they will never forget. 'A sublimely funny book . . . unforgettable and universal' Candia McWilliam

**Sons and Lovers**   D. H. Lawrence

Gertrude Morel, a delicate yet determined woman, no longer loves her boorish husband and devotes herself to her sons, William and Paul. Inevitably there is conflict when Paul falls in love and seeks to escape his mother's grasp. Lawrence's modern masterpiece reflects the transition between the past and the future, between one generation and the next, and between childhood and adolescence.

**Cold Comfort Farm**   Stella Gibbons

When the sukebind is in the bud, orphaned, expensively educated Flora Poste descends on her relatives at Cold Comfort Farm. There are plenty of them – Amos, called by God; Seth, smouldering with sex; and, of course, Great Aunt Ada Doom, who saw 'something nasty in the woodshed' . . . 'Very probably the funniest book ever written' Julie Burchill, *Sunday Times*

# READ MORE IN PENGUIN

*Published or forthcoming:*

**A Confederacy of Dunces**  John Kennedy Toole

A monument to sloth, rant and contempt, a behemoth of fat, flatulence and furious suspicion of anything modern – this is Ignatius J. Reilly of New Orleans. In magnificent revolt against the twentieth century, he propels his monstrous bulk among the flesh-pots of a fallen city, a noble crusader against a world of dunces. 'A masterwork of comedy' *The New York Times*

**Giovanni's Room**  James Baldwin

Set in the bohemian world of 1950s Paris, *Giovanni's Room* is a landmark in gay writing. David is casually introduced to a barman named Giovanni and stays overnight with him. One night lengthens to more than three months of covert passion in his room. As he waits for his fiancée to arrive from Spain, David idealizes his planned marriage while tragically failing to see Giovanni's real love.

**Breakfast at Tiffany's**  Truman Capote

It's New York in the 1940s, where the Martinis flow from cocktail-hour to breakfast at Tiffany's. And nice girls don't, except, of course, Holly Golightly. Pursued by Mafia gangsters and playboy millionaires, Holly is a fragile eyeful of tawny hair and turned-up nose. She is irrepressibly 'top banana in the shock department', and one of the shining flowers of American fiction.

**Delta of Venus**  Anaïs Nin

In *Delta of Venus* Anaïs Nin conjures up a glittering cascade of sexual encounters. Creating her own 'language of the senses', she explores an area that was previously the domain of male writers and brings to it her own unique perceptions. Her vibrant and impassioned prose evokes the essence of female sexuality in a world where only love has meaning.

# READ MORE IN PENGUIN

**A Clockwork Orange**   Anthony Burgess

Fifteen-year-old Alex enjoys rape, drugs and Beethoven's Ninth. He and his gang rampage through a dystopian future, hunting for terrible thrills, until he finds himself at the mercy of the state and the ministrations of Dr Brodsky, the government psychologist. *A Clockwork Orange* is both a virtuoso performance from an electrifying prose stylist and a serious exploration of the morality of free will.

**On the Road**   Jack Kerouac

*On the Road* swings to the rhythms of 1950s underground America, with Sal Paradise and his hero Dean Moriarty, traveller and mystic, the living epitome of Beat. Now recognized as a modern classic, its American Dream is nearer that of Walt Whitman than F. Scott Fitzgerald, and it goes racing towards the sunset with unforgettable exuberance, poignancy and autobiographical passion.

**Zazie in the Metro**   Raymond Queneau

Impish, foul-mouthed Zazie arrives in Paris from the country to stay with her female-impersonator Uncle Gabriel. All she really wants to do is ride the metro, but finding it shut because of a strike, Zazie looks for other means of amusement and is soon caught up in a comic adventure that becomes wilder and more manic by the minute. Queneau's cult classic is stylish, witty and packed full of wordplay and phonetic games.

**Lolita**   Vladimir Nabokov

Poet and pervert Humbert Humbert becomes obsessed by twelve-year-old Lolita and seeks to possess her, first carnally and then artistically. This seduction is one of many dimensions in Nabokov's dizzying masterpiece, which is suffused with a savage humour and rich verbal textures. 'You read Lolita sprawling limply in your chair, ravished, overcome, nodding scandalized assent' Martin Amis

# READ MORE IN PENGUIN

*Published or forthcoming:*

**Seven Pillars of Wisdom**  T. E. Lawrence

Although 'continually and bitterly ashamed' that the Arabs had risen in revolt against the Turks as a result of fraudulent British promises, Lawrence led them in a triumphant campaign. *Seven Pillars of Wisdom* recreates epic events with extraordinary vividness. However flawed, Lawrence is one of the twentieth century's most fascinating figures. This is the greatest monument to his character.

**A Month in the Country**  J. L. Carr

A damaged survivor of the First World War, Tom Birkin finds refuge in the village church of Oxgodby where he is to spend the summer uncovering a huge medieval wall-painting. Immersed in the peace of the countryside and the unchanging rhythms of village life, Birkin experiences a sense of renewal. Now an old man, he looks back on that idyllic summer of 1920.

**Lucky Jim**  Kingsley Amis

Jim Dixon has accidentally fallen into a job at one of Britain's new redbrick universities. A moderately successful future beckons, as long as he can survive a madrigal-singing weekend at Professor Welch's, deliver a lecture on 'Merrie England' and resist Christine, the hopelessly desirable girlfriend of Welch's awful son Bertrand. 'A flawless comic novel . . . It has always made me laugh out loud' Helen Dunmore, *The Times*

**Under Milk Wood**  Dylan Thomas

As the inhabitants of Llareggub lie sleeping, their dreams and fantasies deliciously unfold. Waking up, their dreams turn to bustling activity as a new day begins. In this classic modern pastoral, the 'dismays and rainbows' of the imagined seaside town become, within the cycle of one day, 'a greenleaved sermon on the innocence of men'.